Farming the Wind

written by
Susan VanderVeen

pictures by
Betsy V. Rutz

AuthorHouse™ LLC
1663 Liberty Drive
Bloomington, IN 47403
www.authorhouse.com
Phone: 1-800-839-8640

This book is printed on acid-free paper.

Because of the dynamic nature of the Internet, any web addresses or links contained in this book may have changed since publication and may no longer be valid. The views expressed in this work are solely those of the author and do not necessarily reflect the views of the publisher, and the publisher hereby disclaims any responsibility for them.

Published by AuthorHouse: 02/20/2014

ISBN: 978-1-4918-4326-0 (sc)
ISBN: 978-1-4918-4325-3 (e)

Library of Congress Control Number: 2014902082

To my indefatigable husband and Windmill Man, Rich.
- S.P.V.
To all future Frannys.
-B.V.R.

An old white farmhouse sits on a hillside with a red barn and lots of little outbuildings. Grand old maple trees stand close together, forming a tunnel over the gravel road with their overhanging branches. The branches toss in the wind all year, in the summer making the road shady, and in the fall they are the prettiest colors of yellow and red. Sometimes when the leaves begin to drop and no car or truck has driven by yet, the road is a carpet of colors just like the trees above it. This is the farm where Franny lives with her mama and papa and her older brother, Jess. Jess is in high school and is on the swim team. Their mother is a science teacher at the middle school. Their father is a farmer.

Franny is in the third grade
and rides the yellow school bus that looks
pretty on the road with the big maple trees.
Franny talks to her papa every morning after
Jess and Mama leave for school. Her bus comes by a
little later and she likes that special time when it is
just the two of them. Papa comes in from milking
and drinks his coffee while Franny finishes her breakfast.
She often asks about any new calves they might have, and
he always answers that they are happy and healthy. Then he
tells Franny what he will be working on that day and she talks
about school and her friends.
It isn't a large farm. They have about forty milk cows, fields
of alfalfa and corn and sometimes soybeans. Papa drives a
tractor that pulls a plow, a harrow, and a manure spreader,
and he spends a lot of time fixing the old machines when they
break down. He is gentle to his cows and their pretty little black
and white calves. Franny knows he is a good farmer, but he shakes
his head a lot and she knows that means he is worrying.

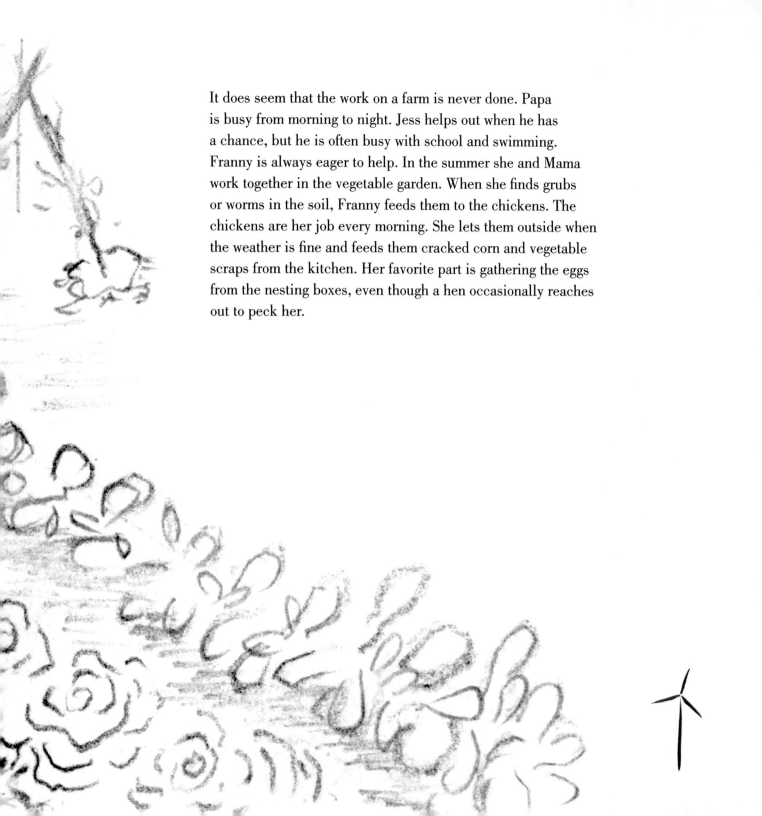

It does seem that the work on a farm is never done. Papa is busy from morning to night. Jess helps out when he has a chance, but he is often busy with school and swimming. Franny is always eager to help. In the summer she and Mama work together in the vegetable garden. When she finds grubs or worms in the soil, Franny feeds them to the chickens. The chickens are her job every morning. She lets them outside when the weather is fine and feeds them cracked corn and vegetable scraps from the kitchen. Her favorite part is gathering the eggs from the nesting boxes, even though a hen occasionally reaches out to peck her.

On weekend mornings, Papa and Mama sit at the kitchen table and talk about the farm while they drink coffee. They talk about the price of milk, the weather, and how much longer the old pickup truck might last. Mama says she could add to her flock of a dozen chickens, but then they laugh about the price of eggs and both of them shake their heads.

On a sunny Saturday in October, Franny was sitting in the sun with a little gray and white barn kitten on her lap. Papa came quickly down the road in his truck, the dust scooting out from behind the tires. When he stopped the truck he jumped out and kissed Franny on the top of her head.

"Where's your mama?" he asked, and not stopping for an answer, he took the back steps up to the kitchen door. Franny followed him inside, leaving the kitten to stretch in the sun. Papa was twirling his arms about as he talked excitedly to Mama about windmills.

Franny listened to him for a moment and then broke in,
"Papa, we have a windmill."
Their old windmill used to pump water but it was no longer
connected to the pump and just rattled and whirred
in the wind.

"But Franny," Papa began,
"do you remember that field of giant wind turbines
way south of here? We never got very close, but
remember how huge they looked? They look different
from our old guy, but it's the same idea. The blades
catch the wind and do the work. They don't pump
water; instead they produce electricity!"

"But Papa," Franny said,
"we already have electricity!"
"That's right, Pumpkin, and so this electricity would be for everyone.
It would be sold to the power company," Papa explained.
Both Franny and her mama looked confused. So Papa went on to say,
"I don't know much more than what I've told you, but the Windmill Man is
coming out early next week. He'll be able to answer your questions.
And mine too!"

Back outdoors, the kitten was gone, and so Franny went to the barn and took
out her bike. She hadn't ridden it for awhile and it was dusty, but the tires were
full and she rode out to the old windmill. It was pretty quiet, as the afternoon was
hardly breezy.
The tower that held the blades was rusty but sturdy.
"You're pretty big yourself," she said to the windmill as she put her head back and
looked all the way up.
The few remaining blades rattled in answer and Franny smiled.

When Franny jumped down from the school bus on
that next Monday afternoon, she saw a strange car in
the driveway. Mama was home but no one was in the
house. Instead, Franny saw a note on the table, held
down with the salt shaker. It said,
"Franny we are out in the alfalfa field with the
Windmill Man."
Franny dropped her backpack and raced out the door.
As she reached the field, she saw the group of three in the
distance. She suddenly felt shy and slowed to a walk. The
Windmill Man was smiling and he had a nice white beard,
but he was talking so fast, and she wasn't sure what he was
trying to explain. Mama and Papa were listening and nodding
their heads, and Franny was glad to see them smiling. The
Windmill Man continued to talk and they all began to walk
back toward the house. The man took some papers from a
notebook to explain something to Papa but the wind tried to
grab them, so Papa asked him into the kitchen and Mama
started some fresh coffee.

"You have questions, don't
you, Franny?" the Windmill
Man asked.
"I know they're big, but tell me
how big," she asked.
"I'll tell you, but I can't wait to show you," he
began. "The turbines that we want to put up here,
they're about the size of maybe ten or twelve houses on top
of each other."
Franny's eyes widened. "That's tall," she said softly, and then
she added, "but also, why do you want to put them up here on our
farm?"
"Good question! It's because you have great wind here, and as long
as the blades turn, electricity is being produced. But it isn't just your
farm we are interested in. A large part of this county is just right for a
big wind project. The electricity will be bought by the power company
and your folks will get paid for having wind turbines on their land."
Finally Franny understood why Papa and Mama were so excited. It seemed like
they were always concerned about money. Getting paid would be good.

But Franny had another question that seemed so
important and no one had mentioned it.
"Papa," she began slowly, hoping it was okay to ask,
"I thought you liked to be a farmer."
Papa swooped her up and gave her a giant hug.
"You're right, Kiddo," and he smiled.
"That's the best part. We get to keep on farming.
The wind turbines take only a small piece of land.
The electric lines are buried, and we get to grow
crops all around them."

This was a lot to think about.
Papa left the house to check on a new calf,
telling Franny that he wanted to make sure
the wee one was happy and healthy. As Papa
walked to the barn, Franny considered all she had
learned about this new project, and she asked the
next logical question,
"When do we get them?"

The Windmill Man smiled and then laughed softly before he went on to explain. He told her about meetings they would be having, and then experts visiting the land looking for the best spots. And finally the ground would have to be prepared for the new turbines.

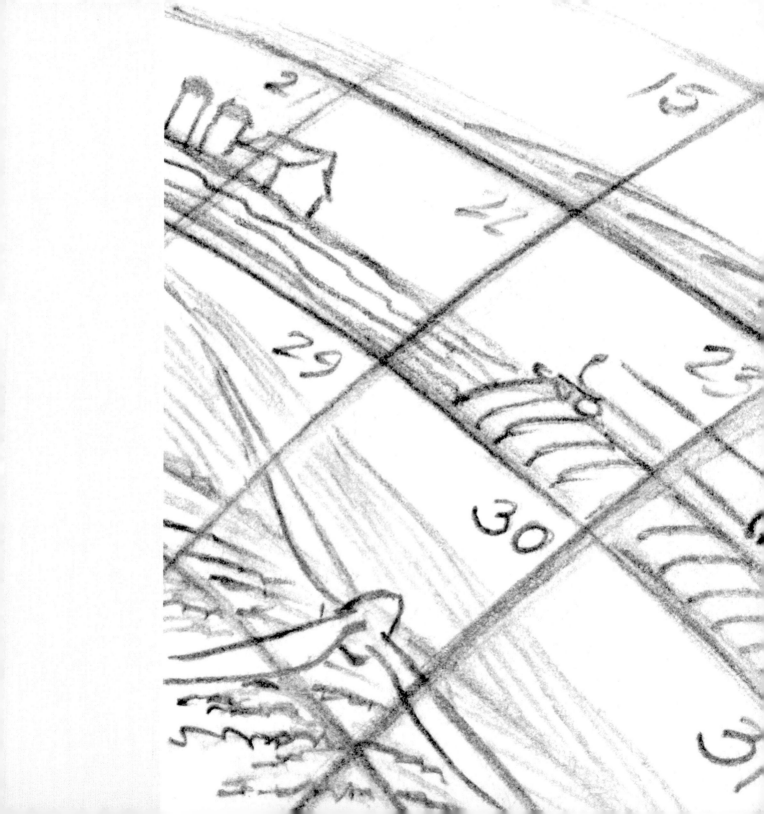

"Franny,"
he hesitated and then went on,
"it will be at least two years before they
are up and running."

Mama was working on dinner in
the kitchen. Franny sat on the back porch
with the Windmill Man, who had been invited
to eat with them.
Jess arrived home from an extra swim practice
and Franny excitedly told him the news.

"Here? Wow! That is so cool," Jess said.

Franny felt a warm spot in her belly as Jess began to talk with
the Windmill Man. She hadn't been certain about the
project until her big brother gave his approval.

"Hey, I'm really glad to hear how you feel about the project,"
the Windmill Man said to Jess.

"Not everyone is as excited as you seem to be."

"Yeah, well, that's because they are kind of weird looking,"
Jess said.

"But electricity with no pollution?!
I call that beautiful!"

Franny had been listening to this conversation and
now she spoke up.

"You know, Jess," she began,

"Papa is a really good farmer, right?"

Her big brother nodded his head and said,

"Sure, he's a good farmer. Why?"

"Well, I just thought," Franny said slowly, "he has the cows and the corn and the alfalfa, and now he'll be farming the wind."
Jess looked at his little sister and laughed, but the Windmill Man threw up his hands and looked pleased.
"You understand it beautifully, Franny," he said. "It's a crop and your father will be its farmer!"
Papa was coming back from the barn and Franny ran to meet him while Jess and the Windmill Man talked. She grabbed his hand and asked how the new calf was doing.
"Happy and healthy," he said as they walked along. And then Franny continued, "Papa, I'm excited about this new adventure!" A little breeze kicked up some dust in the driveway and Franny squeezed Papa's hand.
"I guess that in a couple years I'll be asking how the calves and new windmills are doing, and maybe,"
He smiled down at her and together they said,
"happy and healthy!"

Epilogue

For the next many months Franny became familiar with waiting.
Waiting for this meeting or the next, waiting for a wind study, a ground water study,
a bird and a bat study. There was waiting to talk to neighbors at long boring meetings
and waiting for the pie at the end of those meetings. But all of the meetings and waiting
were heading them in the right direction, toward a wind farm that would serve the
community and benefit the families.

After all of the surveying was complete and the sites were chosen, then it was time for the
foundations to be dug. Franny watched as each fifty foot diameter hole was dug, about ten
feet deep. Then she watched as fifty tons of steel pipe, called rebar, was carefully laid in
the hole. The long anchor bolts were placed in the foundations and then the forty cement
trucks began arriving to fill each of the foundations with 380 tons of concrete.

She and Jess rode their bikes along the dusty roads and watched as the trenches
were dug for the heavy cables that carry the electricity. The trenches were four to five
feet deep, so the cables would not be in the way of the farm machinery that is used for
plowing and planting and harvesting crops.

Although Franny had paid close attention to the huge holes in the ground and then changes
to the roads for the incoming towers, she wasn't prepared for the enormous trucks that brought
not only the turbine parts, but also the huge cranes used to erect them. It took ten long trucks
to bring the parts for each turbine. There was a blade on each of three trucks, the hub on
another, and the nacelle on a fifth. The nacelle holds the generator that converts the wind
energy into electricity, and it is bigger than a school bus. The towers were made up of five
sections, each of these arriving separately. Franny and Jess walked down the icy roads to
several of the sites to watch the colossal equipment used to erect the giants.

At long last, as winter turned to spring, and Franny was almost finished with fifth grade,
the project began to speed up. The towers were erected and the blades were put in place.
The connections were made and the turbines were on line. The wind continued to blow,
and ever so slowly, those blades began to turn.

As the years passed the turbines continued to turn slow and steady and folks
came to love that beautiful ridge of windmills.

Understanding Wind Power

Why do we want wind power?

Everyone uses electricity. Whenever we turn on a light or a computer, use a TV or a refrigerator, we are using it. In fact, anything we plug in uses electricity. The electricity comes from different sources, and the wind is one of them. It is becoming more popular throughout the world because it is safe and does not pollute. Also, wind energy is renewable, which means that it does not get used up.

However, the wind does not always blow, so it is necessary that the power companies have other sources for their electricity.

How does it work?

When a wind turbine works, the electricity that it makes goes into the supply that the power company has, which is called the grid. The power company provides the electricity to its customers from the grid and then the customers pay for it. So when we use electricity provided by our power company, some of it is made by wind power.

A closer look at the turbines:

Wind turbines come in different sizes, and many of them are enormous. Some of the big ones reach more than 300 feet into the air, and their blades are over 100 feet long. The blades and the hub, where they meet, is called the rotor. The sweep that a large rotor makes will be well over 200 feet.

The hub of the turbine is attached to the nacelle, which sits on top of the tower. The nacelle is huge, bigger than a school bus, and it is the unit that holds the gearbox and the generator, which converts the wind energy into electricity.

Construction:

Because of their great size, the job of erecting wind turbines is a very big one. It takes many people with all kinds of expertise to get the job done. For a large turbine, they will dig a hole 50 feet in diameter, at least eight feet deep. The hole is filled with steel rods called rebar, which strengthens the concrete that then fills the hole. This is the turbine's foundation. There are large anchor bolts within this foundation that keep the tower in place.

The tower comes in three or four sections, each one arriving on a giant truck bed. The sections are erected by enormous cranes. Finally the nacelle, along with the blades and the hub are lifted and fit into place. The size of these machines, both the cranes and the turbines, is awesome, and the construction is a wonder to watch.

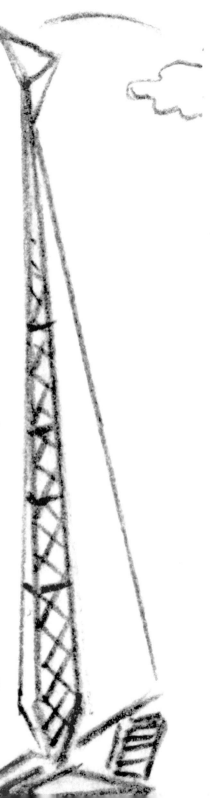

Hub
Nacelle

Blade

Tower.
Ladder
in tower
has over
360 steps.

There are trenches that are dug for the heavy cables that carry the electricity. These trenches are four or five feet beneath the ground, out of the way of farming equipment, so that when the tower is up and the cables have been buried, the only change to the farm is a small access road to the turbines and the tall turbines themselves.

Wind turbines are huge and very expensive. The average life for a turbine is twenty years, and then it can be removed or replaced. If a wind turbine is decommissioned because of age or it is being replaced by a newer model, the materials from the old turbine can be recycled.

Jobs:

A wind power development is a good employer! The developers of a project work with many experts to determine the best spots for the turbines. This may include meteorologists, geologists, and biologists. Then they need to have the land prepared before the turbines are delivered. There are lots of people involved in this work. Roads may need to be built or widened. And there are experts who make the foundation and bury the cables, others who deliver the large components, and even more who erect the giant towers. There are also people specially trained to work with the blades and the gearbox, who will solve problems that may occur. Part of this training involves climbing the tall turbines and learning to work far off the ground.

Concerns with wind turbines:

For many people, their first concern with wind power is the potential danger that the turbines impose upon wildlife, especially birds and bats. This is an issue that has been and continues to be studied by scientists in order to lessen the danger the turbines might impose. Wind developers are generally people who care deeply about the health of the planet. Along with scientists, they continue to study the best practices in order to make wind power safe for our earth. Changes to the turbines and careful placement of the towers continues to reduce problems that might otherwise occur. All of this is happening in order to produce the energy that we all need as a clean resource.

There are many publications and websites that have very detailed and up-to-date information about wind power. Listed here are some helpful websites:

www.nrel.gov
www.awwi.org
www.truthaboutwindpower.com

CPSIA information can be obtained
at www.ICGtesting.com
Printed in the USA
383328LV00003B/11

9781491843260